A Portal Through Time

By

Kayla Renee

A Portal Through Time

Text copyright 2022 by Kayla Renee

This is a work of fiction

Cover artist: Leisa (germancreative)

Published by Kayla Renee

Fantasy, Time Travel.

"Consider this. We all see the world through different eyes. We all remain people, though we see things differently." - Kayla Renee

The sunset made Ethan squint as he stepped off the porch step into the early evening. The sun threw shadows through the trees, painting the sky a pale pink. He bounded down the porch and took off towards the barn that stood dark against the setting sun. He slipped through the doors and hurried to where his horse, Frank, was impatiently clopping in his stall.

Ethan reached out to unlatch the lock when a hand slipped over his mouth. He struggled before turning and seeing Scout standing behind him, dropping her hand and grinning as she stuffed her hands into her jeans pockets.

"Good gosh, Scout! Don't do that!" Ethan exclaimed.

"I've already got Molly ready! She's out back," Scout said casually, smiling.

"Your parents won't miss you?"

"What if they do?" She wriggled her eyebrows at him.

Ethan stared at her scruffy brown hair, which was coated with dirt and dust.

"Okay, I don't get you." He opened the door and stepped inside, urging Frank out of the stall. "How far tonight?"

"As far as they'll take us!" Scout grabbed his arm, leaning against him for a moment before skipping ahead, opening the back door of the barn for Ethan and Frank. Molly nickered as Frank was led out, the two bumping noses in the dusky, summer evening.

"Maybe they're in love," Scout said as she gripped Molly's mane and swung herself up bareback.

Ethan snorted, mounting Frank and bringing him up beside Scout. He could barely make out her face, but he could tell she was studying him. He looked away and nudged Frank's side. Frank began walking, Molly catching up next to them. The comforting sound of hooves on dirt, no saddles creaking, soothed Ethan as he let his weight shift based on Frank's stride. He heard Scout urge Molly to go faster. He grinned and did the same to his horse. They now trotted along.

"You wanna go?" Scout asked.

He heard eagerness in her voice, making his stomach flip flop. "Always," he said, grinning.

They simultaneously alerted their horses, and Molly and Frank transitioned to a gallop. Across the prairie in the dim light they raced, getting nearer and nearer to the pink sky in the distance.

"Molly will beat Frank this time!" Scout called, her voice snatched away in the wind.

"Oh, no, she won't!" He leaned forward, taking a deep breath. The horsey, musty, dirty smell filled his nostrils. Frank's mane whipped his face as they sped up, the horse's neck muscles tightening slightly as he strained to keep ahead of Molly, who was incredibly fast.

Ethan felt the wind whip his hair, and that feeling of being free filled him, making him want to laugh as if he were a child again, as if he were riding his pony, trotting along, Scout right behind him. Frank's breathing became heavier as he gave one more burst of speed, his strong legs taking longer strides. Ethan turned his head, seeing Scout neck and neck with him as she clutched Molly's mane with both hands, leaning forward and looking straight ahead. She looked at Ethan, making eye contact for a split second, breaking into a grin over her freckled face. He looked forward again, determined not to let her distract him, no matter how his stomach fluttered. He gave Frank a nudge with his feet. Frank strained his legs, stretching them as far forward as they'd go.

Scout screamed. Ethan ignored her, assuming she was trying to distract him. She had done that before. But then he heard a thump, as if Molly had stumbled. Scout hollered.

He sat up, intending to turn Frank around when a flash of light blinded him. Scout screamed again. Frank stumbled but still ran. Ethan tugged at his horse's mane to signal him to turn around.

"Go back!" he screamed at Frank. He felt Frank's muscles tighten as the horse tried to turn, but something seemed to be propelling the horse forward, forward, ever forward.

A frightening magnetic force pulled at Ethan's head, enveloping his whole body in the pull, Frank along with him. The light started shimmering, Frank's legs still moving as if he could not slow down. Shapes started forming in the light, an outline of a large city, larger than Ethan had ever seen before. His heart pounded against his chest as the city disappeared in the magnificent light. The two were now floating in the light, but Ethan could still hear Frank's hooves pounding on the dirt, hear his horse's breath come out in puffs, feel the mane on his face.

A green landscape sprung to life all around him, the sun just peeking above trees to his left and drawing an early morning. He was in an open park. Frank stopped, breathing heavily. Ethan clutched Frank's neck, feeling his pulse in his throat. Noises filled the air; they sounded like cars, but they hummed quietly. The quiet countryside he knew had vanished.

He slowly sat up, Frank nervously thumping a foot on the grass. Ethan noticed the foam dripping from his mouth. He gave his horse an uneasy pat, looking around. People walked along neat patches here and there, their clothes strange - brightly colored, clean, no rips, no messy hair. Looking to his right, a big city loomed. Glass buildings illuminated by the sun that steadily rose in the sky.

"Okay, buddy," Ethan said, turning the horse around, half expecting to see the familiar field behind them. Scout would be sitting astride Molly, grinning wickedly at him with a *Haha! I got you good* expression playing on her face.

She wasn't there. Just the grassy field surrounded by neatly trimmed trees.

"Scout?" Ethan called, ears yearning for an answer. A laugh. Anything. He got nothing. Nothing at all except for the occasional horn blast in the distance. A drip of sweat ran down his forehead. He swiveled Frank around again, trying to breathe deeply.

"Okay." He slid off Frank's back, going over and using his handkerchief to wipe the horse's foaming mouth. He shoved the disgusting piece of cloth back into his pocket and held the horse's nose. "It's gonna be okay," he said. His hands shook as he stepped away from Frank, looking into his eyes.

A loud noise made Frank's eyes widen, whiteness filling them. He reared, hoof making contact with Ethan's head and pushing him over. Ethan's star-struck vision saw a shadow leaping over him, felt the vibrations of Frank's hooves in the grass, then blackness.

He opened his eyes, light blinding him again, ears ringing. A hand felt his forehead. He turned his head, not wanting whoever was there to keep their hand on his forehead. He moaned, stirring.

"You okay? You were knocked out."

"Unconscious?" he asked, sitting up blearily.

The woman in front of him had wavy blond hair and shockingly blue eyes - no, they were green-purple. *What?* They changed color. He stared for a moment. Her bright clothing made his eyes sore. "Where am I?" he asked, blinking away his bewilderment.

The woman furrowed her eyebrows. "New York. How did you get here, sweetie?"

"Don't call me that." She made him uneasy. Where was Scout? This woman was a good ten years older than him. Maybe in her early thirties.

"My apologies. What's your name?" She put a hand on his shoulder.

He shrugged it off, getting the urge to scoot away from this woman. Something wasn't right. "Ethan," he said, looking around nervously. "Where's New York?"

"Excuse me?" The woman's eyes flashed red for a second, before returning to the blue they had been at before.

"Why do your eyes –"

"Honey, where are you from?" Her eyes changed again.

Ethan slowly scooted away from her. She tried getting close to him, eyes concentrating on his face.

"I-" His mind blanked. This strange place was so loud. He stood up.

"Honey, are you sure you can-"

He turned and ran. He sprinted to the sidewalk and down it, making his way to the city. Maybe Scout was there. Maybe this was all a prank she had come up with. She would come out of a building laughing, and they would be back racing Frank and Molly. It would be okay.

The sounds grew louder as he entered the city. He stopped and stared. The cars didn't have wind-ups on the front. The cars were *floating* right above the road. People were everywhere in bright-colored clothes, things flashing in front of their faces like a projection. Dings and pings rang abundantly. People talked loudly and quickly.

His eyes scanned the streets where stands were set up. Moving metal arms handed people things as they gave bills to slots, automatic, humanoid voices coming from everywhere. His heart rate sped up.

He turned to see a robotic face right behind him. He leapt back, bumping into someone who spoke a word he did not care to repeat.

"Identification," the bot-human voice said.

"I-" Ethan looked around. Other robots walked around, exchanging things with people.

"Identification. You do not possess any electronics. I must get your identification."

"Electronics?"

"A newbie?" a girl's voice asked.

He looked around. A girl with long brown hair and highlights stared at him. Her eyes were a sapphire rainbow, the color pigmentation was unbelievable.

"Identification, please." The robot's eyes turned red, and it took a step closer to Ethan.

Ethan stepped back, looking at the girl again. Her bright red dress set her frame nicely.

"You aren't from around here, are you?" She pressed her left temple, and a little red line shot into Ethan's head.

He ducked, falling to the ground.

"It's okay, I'm just getting your profile from you. You don't seem to have one, though." Her eyebrows scrunched. She leaned forward and helped him up.

Ethan shook his head. "My profile? My identification? What?"

"Trouble," the robotic figure said.

"Oh, shut up," the girl said, turning and shoving the robot away.

"Reporting, reporting, reporting." The robot left, flashing red.

"Where?" Ethan's mind whirled with all the new things going on. "Where's Scout?"

"Who?" the girl asked.

"Scout, you know her?"

She shook her head. "No, I'm Eliza. Who are you?" She smiled, and her eyes flashed a vibrant purple.

"What's with your eyes?" he blurted out.

She smiled, and they turned yellow, reminding him of the light that had somehow dragged him here. "It's the newest thing! Isn't it fantastic?" she said, her voice becoming higher pitched, excitement emanating from her.

"You can get it imprinted too! Come!" She grabbed his wrist.

"Wha–?" His world swam. Electricity buzzed through him and vibrated his blood cells. "What?" He ripped his wrist out of hers.

Her eyes turned dark blue. He could see waves crashing onto the beach in them.

"It's okay. It doesn't hurt." She ran her fingers through his hair as if they had known each other forever.

He stumbled back, falling on his tailbone and wincing. "I don't understand what's going on." He scrambled to his feet.

Eliza tapped her wrist, and her hair was pulled back into a ponytail. Ethan had seen Scout pull her hair back, but she never tapped her wrist to do it. She would use both hands and smoothe her hair back and-

"Let's get you all pampered," Eliza said, her eyes gleaming. "You need some upgrades. You look like you've never had a phone."

"Phone?"

She took another step toward him.

"No," He brushed past her and ran.

"Boy!" she screeched.

He weaved in and out of people, trying to outrun the strangeness of it all. He stumbled, catching himself on a lamppost that glowed yellow at his touch. He recoiled from it, stumbling into a woman who had a floating orb in front of her. A baby cried, its noise muffled inside the sphere. He turned to stare as the woman tapped some buttons.

"Sorry."

The woman merely glanced at him instead of giving him a whooping. A boy about his age glided along, making Ethan take a double look at his shoes. They seemed to be gliding along the ground as if they had wheels. The boy glanced at him, then halted.

"Bro, what?" He stared at Ethan. Ethan stepped back. The boy's eyes visibly focused, concentric circles forming around his iris, moving mechanically. "How do you have no profile?"

Ethan shook his head, body trembling like a leaf.

"There you are!" a girl squealed, clutching his arm as if she were Scout. Ethan saw Eliza giving him a giddy grin. He tried jerking out of her grip, but her fingers tightened on his arms. Her voice was unnervingly high-pitched. "Let's go to the center!"

"Let's not. I don't know who - *what* you people are!" He fought against the girl's grip. The dude shrugged and gilded onwards.

"It's Ethan, isn't it?" the girl asked, flinging her arm around his shoulders.

"How?" Ethan asked, too shocked that she knew his name to bother shrugging her off.

"It's part of my upgrade." She giggled, the sound echoing through the streets. She started walking, and Ethan followed automatically, somewhat entranced, even with all the bleeping sounds driving him bonkers. Her arm around his shoulder prominent in his mind. She led him down several streets, faster than the normal person would usually walk. They entered a large square.

"This is where the White House used to be," she said, pointing to the glass building that loomed over them.

"Used to?" he asked, looking at her.

Her pupils were now a mash of rainbow colors, billowing like storm clouds. "I know, right? Now that the Errats control America, everything has changed! The white

House used to be in Washington, but it makes so much more sense to be in New York."

"The what now? Makes more sense?"

"Honestly, you don't read the news, do you?" She dragged him on, up the flight of glass steps, under which fish swam. How, he couldn't tell, and through the glass doors they went. The inside was a large arc of glass windows. The white tiled floor led to a desk that was a glowing tank full of fish. The desk attendant - no, a metal human – looked up as Eliza dragged Ethan to the desk.

"Identification."

"May scan," Eliza said, letting Ethan go for a moment and standing straight.

The humanoid blinked. "Eliza Pevington. Seventeen. Resident of New York. Social Security Number 457-28-1040."

Eliza bounced on her feet. "That's me!"

"Wha? How did it just-"

The robot turned to him. Ethan stepped back.

"It's okay, E." she said, letting out that high-pitched laugh that made his neck hairs stand up. "He's just going to make sure you aren't a dummy." She chortled. Ethan looked at the robot as it blinked.

"No identification. Must be fixed. Take to door 557 for identification."

"Thanks, Gen!" Eliza squealed to the robot.

"See you later, 1040." It turned away. Ethan started backing up, eyes roaming the white doors that led nowhere.

Eliza grabbed his arm and skipped to the door that was labeled 557. No one was in line.

"Go on," Eliza said. "Knock!" She nodded.

He looked from her to the door. He shook his head. "I don't know where I am."

"Yes, you do!" She squeezed his arm.

"No." He turned to her. "Where did all this stuff come from?"

"What do you mean?" she asked, her smile faltering.

"I - when was all this…this…built?" Ethan stuttered.

"I dunno. Thirty-five years ago? Why should I care? It was before I was born." She shrugged like it did not matter.

Ethan's pulse raced. "N-no. Because I went to New York with my family three years ago and - and it wasn't this."

"Three years ago? You must have bad eyesight."

"No, Eliza, I promise. I was here." He put his hand in his hair.

"You -" A strange expression crossed her face. "Ethan."

He looked at her, surprised by the change in her voice.

"What?" he snapped.

"What year is it?"

"1775. Why?"

Eliza's pupils turned all white, then a greenish blue. "You got amnesia?"

"Um...no..."

"Am I imagining you?"

"Uh..."

"Slap me."

"What?"

"Slap me!"

Ethan hesitated.

"Now," she said, preparing herself, eyes turning a stony gray.

Ethan slapped her. The first time he had ever slapped a girl. His hand stung. Eliza turned back to him, her mouth open.

"Ow," she said, Ethan cringed.

"Sorry…"

"I'm not dreaming."

"No," Ethan said. "And I need to get out of this crazy pothole and get back home. I need to find Scout."

"Who's Scout?"

"She's no one," he said, angry at himself for mentioning her. "And I need to find my horse…" He stared over Eliza's shoulder.

"You have a horse? I've never seen a horse here."

"He ran off," Ethan said, wondering what could have happened to him. Where had he gone? "I need to leave now."

"No, you need to at least get upgraded first, please."

"Don't you forget that I'm from 1775, and this is not 1775. I don't know where I am and what all the stupid bleeping is or what is going on with your eyes!"

Her eyes turned a bright pink.

Ethan stepped back. "I got to go find my horse."

"Nah, let's get your stuff first." She knocked on the door.

"No!"

The door opened, and a person in all blue looked out.

"Here for identification!" Eliza piped up. She shoved Ethan through the door.

"No, thank you, I'm good," Ethan said, shuffling his feet back, but Eliza's hands were on his back, pushing him forward.

"It'll be okay!" she assured, the highlighted parts of her hair turning a vibrant pink.

He lost track of things for a moment, eyes staring at the pink highlights that had just burst to life. The person in gloves dragged him inside, the door slamming shut behind him.

"I don't need identification," he said, eyes roaming the room. Strange, glass organizers... A chair in the middle of the room... Things he was unable to identify.

The doctor blinked at him. "You have no identification. That's illegal. You must get identification."

"I am already identified," he protested, holding his hands up, pressing himself to the door. "I'm Ethan, see? That's enough."

"Identification needed." This person, whose pupils also changed colors, had eyes that glowed a mix of gray and blue, with red sparks like lightning in them. The strange doctor went over to one of the glass drawers. Ethan turned the handle of the door desperately, but it had somehow locked. He could not budge it. He looked up to see the doctor walking toward him with a vial in her hands. A needle poked out of it.

"No!" He ran to the other side of the room.

"Ethan." The doctor's voice had turned unhuman. "I hate to put you in the chair."

Ethan's eyes snapped to the chair. Something about it made his muscles shake. Ethan shook his head. "I don't need identification...ma'am."

The doctor stopped, eyes turning a misty white.

"Haven't heard that phrase for years... It will do you no good."

The doctor lunged at Ethan. Ethan hurled himself to the left, colliding with one of the weird glass shelves. It shattered on impact, glass raining down on him. The doctor yanked on his ankle, saving him from the rain of glass. She snapped her fingers, and the glass repaired itself immediately.

The doctor jabbed the needle into his temple. A splitting pain filled his head. He screamed. *Things* flashed before his eyes. Words. Lights. People. The robotic human's voice echoed in his head.

How do you identify?

I'm a male, duh.

Logged as: I'm a male, duh. Your social security number is 220-82-4589. Ethan."

The room dissolved back into being. He stared at the ceiling, dazed.

"Well, duh," the doctor said, tossing the needle into the waste bin. "On to the next upgrading system."

"I don't want - whatever it is you've got."

"Of course you do, Ethan," the doctor said, hoisting him up by his shoulders and leading him stiffly to the door.

The person - robot, whatever it was, shoved him out the door.

He stumbled into Eliza. Her hair was back to normal.

"There you are!" her high-pitched voice squeaked. "Isn't it wonderful? Let's go to station two now! You can get eyes like mine!" She blinked exaggeratedly. "Ohhh! Interesting pronouns!"

"Will you all just shut up!" Ethan bellowed. "I don't understand this pronoun thing you all talk about! We are who we are!"

"What do you mean? You can be whatever you want."

"I don't know where you came up with the idea that – I just want to go home."

"Oh, not yet. Wherever you live, you miss out on all the cool stuff. Come on!" She pulled him, struggling, to another door.

"No. Let me go. I have no money!"

"Money? Money! That's so old school! We have cookies now. They're embedded into your temple! Then you don't have to worry about losing them or them getting stolen!"

"Embedded in me? Shots for identification? What is up with your society?"

"Everything is all right, it's okay." She stroked his cheek.

"Stop." He slapped her hand away. She looked hurt, her eyes turning a deep green. "I don't want you. I don't want random things jabbed into me! Why do you think I need it?"

"You are underrating yourself," she cooed.

"I'm not-"

She knocked on a door, her eyes flashing a quick teal.

The door swung open. Ethan shook his head, giving her a warning, but she lurched forward and pushed him into the room. The door slammed shut.

Everything was pink. A bright fuchsia that just about burned his eyes out. He didn't notice the person until she moved. He took a step back.

"Welcome, Ethan."

"H-how do you know-"

"I see we are in need of some upgrades. Not to worry, not to worry." The woman slowly walked towards him, her pink shoes blending into her pink pants, seamlessly going up into her long pink jacket. Her pink hair hung all over her shoulders, pink eyeshadow and eyeliner splattered by her eyes, and her pink lipstick set the whole outfit frighteningly well. The woman's eyes turned a quick shade of blue before reverting to pink.

"What do you want with me?" Ethan asked.

"To help you."

"To - to help me?" His breathing slowed. Some sort of lyricless music was playing, and it appeared to be soothing his racing mind.

"Ah, yes, my son. You have gone through quite some trauma recently. They took away all your rights. They took away all your electronics. We, myself and Eliza outside, are here to rescue you. It's going to be okay."

"It's going to be…okay?" He looked down at his hands that were still dirty from his horse. A faint flicker of regret flashed through him, some sort of concern nagging in his stomach. "Okay."

"Sit in your chair here, Ethan. You'll feel better in a little bit. You are about to get the newest upgrade first! Free of charge because you came in with nothing and to fit in you must be changed."

"I must be-upgraded…" Ethan's mind slowed, his eyes unfocused for a moment, as if he were sinking into a warm bath, head cushioned on a luxurious pillow.

"It is going to change your world." She brought a pink machine up to his eyes and put it on as if it were a pair of spectacles. She pressed a button.

Light blinded him. It burned his eyes. He tensed, hands clenching the sides of the chair. Scout flashed before his eyes. The woman's voice made it to his ears.

"It's okay honey. Everything is going as it should."

Scout galloped on Molly, her hair flying behind her. His heart ached to be with his friend again, to find Frank and go home. The bright light intensified. Scout's hair turned fuchsia, violet, a light blue, then she puffed out of sight.

"Scout!" he shouted, straining against the machine. "Scout!"

"Everything is as it should be," the woman soothed. "It is all right."

"It's all right." Ethan relaxed, and the light turned pink, green, then a soft yellow, fading away until he realized he was looking at the pink room again.

"What?" He blinked. Everything seemed brighter, more beautiful.

The woman in front of him was stunning. Somehow, he knew her name.

Lacy.

Thirty-seven.

Job: upgrader.

"Isn't that better?" Lacy asked.

He nodded slowly. "Y-yeah." He blinked, and she seemed to glow.

Lacy smiled at him. "You want a phone now?"

"Of course!" he said, jumping out of his seat in the excitement of it all. This strange new place didn't seem so strange anymore. "I'm so ready!" He reached out compulsively and folded the woman's hands in between his.

"Good!" the woman exclaimed. "Now off you go!"

"Thank you, Lacy!" he said, skipping to the door while waving at her.

She gave a grin that, for a moment, made his enthusiasm falter. Something was strange. He burst out the door and bumped into Eliza.

"Ethan," she said, a smile breaking on her face. "Feel better?"

"Loads! I don't know what I was worried about before – woah." He blinked at Eliza. She was different. She seemed to have a slight glow.

"You ready for your phone?" she asked, holding her hand out to him. He took it.

He stared at her, nodding slowly. "Y-yeah."

"Let's go!"

She ran ahead, and he began running with her. They went through the large domed room that had intimidated him at first but now seemed to be marvelous, and of course, the doorways that led nowhere fit there just right. Their footsteps echoed, making a different sound, as if they were running on a piano with each step. A gargled laugh burst from his mouth, combining with Eliza's laughs that no longer annoyed him.

"Ha! This is wonderful!" Ethan declared.

They stopped outside another door.

"This is it!" Eliza said, turning to him, bouncing energetically.

"Yes. See you soon!" He bounded through the door, stopping once through.

The room was white. White floors, hard countertops, like a lab in those black-and-white movies. A gray chair sat in a corner, vials filled with something on the counter. A person in a white coat – he blinked.

Charles.

Forty-seven.

Job: Phone upgrader.

Looking up at him, Charles blinked. "Hello, Ethan."

Ethan looked at his horsey hands, a small feeling of regret flashing through him.

"Hi…" His legs screamed to go back, but they wouldn't move.

"Ready for your upgrade?"

"Uh - uh, yeah."

"Take a seat, Ethan."

Ethan's legs carried him to the chair. "What are you gonna do?"

"Upgrade you, son."

"I'm not your son."

The man stared at him for a moment, then shrugged. "I see you are not from this time zone. You found the time rip." He went to a drawer and started rummaging in it.

"T-time rip?"

"I can see it. You are not from this time. How do you like this century? It's a lot better than the past, isn't it?"

Ethan looked around, not really remembering his past. "Um...yeah." A faint, familiar fear flitted through him, but he blinked, and it was gone.

"Now, this may hurt a little, but it will be over with quickly." Charles slipped on plastic gloves. He took a rag and batted some rubbing alcohol on it. The smell pigmented the room as if he had dumped a whole gallon onto the floor.

Ethan coughed.

"Suppose you ain't used to this stuff being so strong, being used to the country and open air, eh?"

"Open air?" Ethan asked.

"Back in the days when we were not surrounded by tech twenty-four-seven."

"You-" Ethan blinked at Charles as he rubbed the stuff on his temples. "Are you from another time too?"

The man nodded.

"What year?"

"Can't remember. I just remember war. I was in a war. Then - it doesn't matter." He grabbed a vial. The needle on this one was large.

Ethan pressed himself into the seat. "I - I'm not sure I want this anymore-"

"It's fine. This is what you want."

"But you were just saying-"

"Now, now, it's going to be quick."

"No, I don't think I want-"

The needle pressed into his temple, feeling like it went right through his head. He shuddered. Scout's face – her smile filled his brain, along with the warm, contented feeling he had gotten that one day when they lay next to each other in the sun on the prairie grass. She flickered away. His memory began fading. His mind flickered off as a TV turns off. His vision went black.

~

He opened his eyes. A soft ringing filled his ears.

"Better?" a voice echoed in his mind, making it vibrate slightly.

He blinked. Everything was eerily calm. He looked around the room.

Charles leaned against a counter, a sympathetic look on his face.

"The world's always better on the other side, ain't it?"

Ethan blinked, shaking his head. "Whoa." He automatically tapped his wrist, and a screen popped up in front of his eyes like a light that magnetized itself together. When he looked at Charles, information about him blistered to life in his mind, as if he knew him better than Charles knew himself.

Charles.

Forty-seven.

Job: Phone upgrader.

Single.

Last upgrade: 7/10/3035.

Last pay raise: 3030.

Ambition: To go home.

Favorite food: Bananas.

Lives In: New York City - The New.

Address: The New 5789.

Known family: None

Introvert.

Social security number: 700-48-2697.

Times escorted to prison: 0.

"I -" Ethan clutched his head.

"I know. Incredible, isn't it?"

"I didn't ask for this!"

"But now you have it. Isn't it wonderful? Everybody wants one."

"I don't really-"

"Go now, enjoy your new life."

Ethan got up, shaking. He wobbled over to the door and opened it, Eliza looked away from her screen and grinned at Ethan.

"Isn't it wonderful?" she asked. He stared at the information about her that popped up in his mind.

Eliza.

Seventeen.

Single.

Last upgrade: 10/01/3035.

Ambition: To be the best.

Favorite food: Pizza

Lives in: New York City - The New

Address: Popularity 578

Known family: Stepfather

Extrovert.

Social security number: 457-28-1040.

Times escorted to prison: 1.

He stared at the last line, then moved his eyes to meet her.

"You've been to prison?"

"I don't want to talk about it." She turned on her heels and started to leave.

"Hey, but what is it about this place that makes everybody so - so…" *It'll be better when you have it. It'll be okay.* Images flashed through his mind. He followed her out of the building, knowing what street he was on, knowing what street they were headed for. He grabbed her hand, and she turned to him. A tear fell out of the corner of her eye.

"What did you go to prison for?" he asked. People brushed past him. She shook her head. "Tell me. *Tell me!*" *It'll be better when I know.*

The tear slid down her cheek. "Now." He felt his eyes burn red, the color heating his eyelids.

Her eyes turned purple, widening in fright. "I - I went because..." She hid her face in her hands.

He couldn't take it. Something new in him roared in fury. He grabbed her shoulders and gave her a shake.

She looked up at him, shocked. "I went because I didn't want to get upgraded..."

He stood stock still, all thought, all new electronics leaving his mind. His world tinted orange.

"I was forced to go..." she went on.

His eyes flared red. "Like *you* forced me to -" His mind went blank again. *Made me do what, exactly? What was so bad about all this technology? It was useful.*

"I didn't want the upgrades, but for whatever reason I didn't have them… I woke up from an insane dream in the middle of a park…one of the few remaining without upgrades. Something made me fall and…I woke up and someone brought me here…"

Ethan studied her. Something about her was becoming familiar. Her hair rippled brown, then back to the highlighted hair she had had before. He blinked.

"I struggled against the person who led me here, but they just got mad… When I broke several items in the phone upgrader room, they called the cops. They put me to sleep, and when I woke up I was fully upgraded… I have no memory at all of my past life… I mean, of where I was before all this… I don't know for sure where I came from. I want to go home, but this is my home."

"But you love the upgrades so much… You are the one who helped me get them."

"Yes…I am the one who made you get them… I don't know, there was something about you."

"Whoa, we just met."

Her eyes turned orange. "I wasn't implying… You just seemed so familiar."

They headed to the park that wasn't upgraded.

"So you woke up in the same place I did, huh?"

"I guess," she said, shrugging. "I remember screaming and -"

Ethan stopped paying attention. A girl's scream filled his head. He remembered riding a horse. *What is a horse?* They made it to the park and stood, staring.

The breeze tickled his face. "Strange, isn't it? A place with no electronics."

"I need food," she said, starting to turn away.

"Hang on," he said, grabbing her shoulder. Something was in the shadows of the trees on the other side of the park. He started for it.

"What are you doing?" Eliza asked, following him. "We never walk on grass." He started moving faster, hearing her puff as she tried to keep up. "Where are we going?"

He approached the strange creature. It huffed, and he froze.

"Ethan?" Elisa put a hand on his shoulder, but he shrugged it off.

He stepped into the shade where the animal moved its hooves nervously. It had something on its forehead.

"Ah." Eliza took in a sharp breath. The brown animal turned its head to show the horn that protruded out of its head.

"Are they real? A unicorn..." she whispered.

"No..." Ethan said, eyes roaming the creature's body. "It was upgraded."

He held his hand out, touching the large animal's hose. The horn retracted. The animal thumped its front hooves nervously.

"Hey." He tapped his wrist. "What kind of animal is this?" His screen popped up, showing an image of a nearly identical animal. *Horse* was the heading. All body parts were labeled, and the kind of horse it was. "This seems familiar, yet not." He walked around the horse, making his screen disappear, disliking it in front of his face for no reason. "Something... Something's familiar about this."

"For me too...but I can't place it," Eliza said, staring at the horse. She stumbled into Ethan.

"Geez!" Ethan said, turning to her, but he stopped.

Eliza looked up into the face of a black horse, one that had also been upgraded. Its eyes looked at her sadly. The two horses nudged noses, nickering to each other. The two teens watched the horses, something painful going through them. Something familiar…yet not…

"What did this place look like before the upgrades?" Ethan asked.

"I told you. It was upgraded before-"

She stared off at the sky, which was growing dark. The sun had begun to set, darkness raining along the park. Street lamps snapped on.

"Before the upgrades…" She looked back at the horses. "Before the upgrades I… If I didn't want the upgrades at first, I must have been like you…right?" She turned to Ethan. "Right?"

"I suppose… Where did I come from?" He touched his wrist and thought *view profile.* His profile popped up. Under family relations: *none.* "I don't have a family…" He looked at Eliza. "But everyone has somebody…right? Unless…" He squeezed his eyes shut, going through all the people he had recently met. Charles popped up. He didn't have any family either. A phrase he said came back to him: *I'm not from this century either... You found the...*

Ethan took a step back. He walked right up to the first horse and with a strange familiarity grabbed its mane. He hoisted himself up on the horse's back.

"What are you doing?" Eliza wondered.

"Something I've done before...I think..." He felt his cheeks flush with excitement. Something was going to happen. "Come with me. Get on that horse."

"Why would I?"

"Just do it."

"I don't know how."

"Like how I did."

"But-" She reached her hand out, tentatively touching the horse's mane. An odd expression crossed her face. Her hand gripped the horse's mane, and with the ease of having done this every day for years, swung herself up. "How did I do that?"

"I don't know, but I really need to try something. Follow me." He nudged the horse. It started walking.

Eliza gave a little scream as he looked back to see her horse following. The feeling was oddly familiar. He gave the horse a greater kick, and it started galloping. Eliza gasped as her horse came neck and neck with his. When he looked at her, he saw Scout leaning full into Molly, hair flying behind her, a smile crossing her face.

The sun threw a pink painting across the sky, and he was free.

The End

About the author:

I have always enjoyed writing. I have memories of writing stories in composition notebooks and illustrating them with stick-figures and markers when I was younger. After a few false starts, *A Portal Through Time* will be my third book published in 2022. I also had a unique opportunity to co-write and produce *Cold Soul*, a song in collaboration with Ceej Boy. When I am not writing, I enjoy a variety of different interests such as breeding betta fish, juggling, working out, and participating in theater. I am currently in college with a double major in English writing and Theater performance.